Benjamin and Rumblechum

Benjamin and Rumblechum

Travel Stories for Children

Kenna Mary McKinnon
and
Emma Shirley Brinson

Dedication

To Steve and Diane Wild, and Ward Lund (Kenna's children), and to all children the world over. KM To the late Kit and Kathleen Manning who dearly loved Benjamin and encouraged Emma to travel with him after she found him in an ESSO Service Station on the border of England and Wales, and to all the students whom Emma had the privilege of teaching during her thirty-seven year teaching career. EB

Acknowledgements

The authors would like to acknowledge the contribution of Sandy Tritt, who so skillfully edited the first version of this book, and the animals and people who populate the manuscript, such as Freedom the cat (who really exists), and Benjamin the stuffed monkey (who really exists!). Kenna's sister Judith Holmes contributed her knowledge of rodeos and cowboys to the story of Slim and the buckin' bronc. Agent Joanne Kellock first heard of the genesis of this story, after Kenna's dream of the two children, Benjamin, and their travels across the wonderful and great country of Canada. The illustrations were skillfully and wonderfully done by Aniela Abair, who contributed much to the appearance and enjoyment of the book. Last but not least, we acknowledge Regina Williams and her daughter Jamie, the publishers who believed in us and our children's story. God bless us every one.

Contents

Chapter 1

Benjamin and Freedom

"I remember many interesting places," Benjamin the Stuffed Monkey said. "I know. I've traveled."

"I've never traveled." Freedom the calico cat licked one orange paw with a pink tongue.

"Aunt Kathleen found me in England. See the Union Jack pin on the lapel of my jacket? It's the British flag." Benjamin wore buttons and pins from many places on his uniform and his hat, which both said "Esso" on them, like the gas station.

"Aunt Kathleen brought you here. I'm glad, Benjamin."

"Then we traveled to New Zealand. We saw the kiwis."

"Fruit?" Freedom purred. She was teasing Benjamin.

"Birds. Then we went to Singapore. We've traveled all over the world. In England, we saw the *Bobbies* and the *prams* and the *lorries*."

Freedom rolled her eyes. Benjamin was bragging about traveling again.

"I've never traveled." Freedom waved one brown paw at Benjamin.

"I've been to Sri Lanka," Benjamin said. "I've traveled to Banff, Alberta."

He was a small stuffed animal, but he could think and dream, and sometimes even talk—to the right critter, of course.

"I've been to Red Deer, Alberta. And back," Freedom said.

"That's not far. And I say goodbye to you right now."

"Goodbye? Goodbye to me? Your good friend?"

"I know a secret," Benjamin said. "A big secret."

"What?" Freedom's wide yellow eyes stared. She grew very still.

"Aunt Kathleen and Aunt Mary. They're planning a trip."

"Where's the trip?"

"You'll see." Benjamin looked around at the other stuffed animals. "I say be aware."

Freedom watched and waited. "Beware? Is Katie going?"

"Yes."

"Is Jacob going, too?"

"Yes."

"Oh, dear. Both children and the aunts are going with you. And what about me?"

Chapter 2

A Disappointment

Sure enough, the next day after a breakfast of oatmeal and toast, Aunt Mary and Aunt Kathleen said to the children, "Get packed, Katie. Get packed, Jacob. We're going to Ontario."

Ontario is a province in Canada far away from Edmonton, Alberta, where they lived. Rumblechum, their minivan, would take them there. They called their minivan Rumblechum because it made a noise that sounded like Rumblechum, Rumblechum, Rum, Rum, Rum. It had a sign in front that said, Twinkle, Twinkle, Aerostar.

"Where is Ontario, Jacob?" Katie pulled her sweater over her head. It was a cool morning.

Jacob was two years ahead of Katie in school. He knew almost everything. He wore glasses and was ten years old. Freedom, the calico cat, heard them talking. She padded into Katie's bedroom where Benjamin the stuffed monkey lay.

"They are planning a trip." Freedom made sad little noises deep in her throat. "You were right. I hope they'll take me."

"Don't be too sure," Benjamin the Monkey said.

His Esso button shone in the sunlight that poured through the window.

"You go with them everywhere. I want to go, too."

"They're packing. See if you'll fit into their suitcase."

When Katie and Aunt Kathleen came up the stairs after they had lunch, they found Freedom in an open suitcase at the top of the stairs. Freedom's big furry body took up most of the space inside the suitcase.

"Meow." Freedom blinked up at Katie with yellow eyes.

"No, Freedom," Katie said. "You can't come with us."

Poor Freedom, Benjamin thought.

"We love you, Freedom," Aunt Kathleen said. "But you wouldn't be happy on a long trip in our van."

"We'll take Benjamin." Aunt Mary came up the stairs behind them. "Benjamin is a stuffed monkey. He won't mind a long trip. Benjamin won't be a bother."

"Bother? Bother? Benjamin won't be a bother? Would I be a bother? Oh, I'm sad, sad." Freedom bowed her head and soft tears rolled down her face.

The two aunts didn't notice.

Katie looked at Freedom. She lifted Freedom out of the suitcase and patted the calico cat on her soft orange and white head. Then she finished packing.

Freedom sat at the window and watched her family pack Rumblechum. They took a tent. They took sleeping bags and pillows. They took food, an MP3 player, a barbecue, and a lighter. They packed and packed. Then they put Benjamin on the front seat between them, in Katie's backpack, with his head and arms sticking out. They gave a house key to their friend Della. Della and her twelve-year-old, almost grown up daughter, Emily, would look after Freedom, the house and the beautiful garden.

Then the two aunts, Katie, and Jacob kissed Freedom goodbye and drove away in Rumblechum, going Rumblechum, Rumblechum, Rum, Rum, Rum all the way down the road.

Freedom watched them from the upstairs window until they were out of sight.

So Aunt Kathleen, in her floppy hat with the bright yellow flower, who owned Rumblechum the minivan, and Aunt Mary, with her old red sweater and her string of pearls, set off for the Province of Ontario with the two children. Benjamin sat very still between Aunt Mary and Aunt Kathleen in Katie's backpack in the front seat of the van. He tried to wave goodbye to Freedom with his little stuffed arms, until the minivan turned the corner and the old grey house was lost from sight.

Chapter 3

A Calamity

Aunt Mary and Aunt Kathleen—with Katie, Jacob, and Benjamin, but without Freedom—drove in Rumblechum for two days. The aunts took turns driving. At night they camped at campgrounds found alongside the highway or by side roads. Jacob liked to camp. Katie missed her little white bed. But she had to admit camping was an adventure, especially with the two aunts, who were great fun.

They drove across Saskatchewan, a province between Alberta and Manitoba. Saskatchewan is very flat. Rumblechum went Rumblechum, Rumblechum, Rum, Rum, Rum almost all the way to the border of Manitoba. Bright yellow canola fields, wheat fields and farms rolled by. The road was very flat and straight.

They drove through the capital city of Saskatchewan, named Regina. They drove and drove. Finally, they arrived in Maryfield, Saskatchewan. It was very dark with only a few lights glittering from the windows of houses along the side of the road. There was no moon. Stars twinkled overhead, brighter here than in the city.

The needle on the gas gauge pointed to "empty." Rumblechum began to cough. Aunt Kathleen drove up to a gas station on the outskirts of Maryfield.

"Oh," Katie said, waking up from where she was sleeping in the back seat. "Are we there yet?"

"Don't be silly," Jacob, said. "Ontario is a l-o-n-g-g-g way farther than this. This is just S-a-s-k-a-t-c-h-e-w-a-n."

Benjamin the Monkey woke up. He had been dreaming about Freedom. Della and Emily were looking after Freedom at home. It was a good dream. But now Benjamin was worried about himself and Katie and Jacob. Rumblechum's engine sounded odd. And it was very dark.

"Are we out of gas?" Jacob asked.

Rumblechum said, "Cough, cough." Their aunt honked the horn. All the lights were out in the gas station. Aunt Mary covered her ears. "Don't honk the horn, Kathleen. It makes my ears ring. It makes me dizzy. I don't like the horn."

"Someone will come," Aunt Kathleen said.

"Look!" Aunt Mary pointed. "There's a man coming. He has a dog with him—a big dog. We'll ask that man for some gas."

Rumblechum lurched and quit running. Aunt Kathleen tried to start the minivan.

"Oh, no! We're out of gas!" Katie rubbed her eyes and yawned.

"What will we do?" Jacob, said. "It's dark. Will the man know where there is some gas we can borrow or buy?"

The man with the dog stopped. He rubbed his head. In the glare of the headlights and through the glass, his face looked kind.

"Trouble, ladies?" the man said.

The dog said, "Woof, woof."

Benjamin looked at the dog. The dog had a very big mouth. He was not on a leash. The dog came closer. Benjamin could not move. He was only a stuffed animal. He was not real like Freedom and the dog. He was lying partly turned over on his back with his face toward the dog, so he could see the dog's big mouth and the big hairy paws.

Aunt Kathleen and Aunt Mary got out of the van. They left the door open. As they got out of the van, the backpack with Benjamin in it was knocked over. Benjamin fell out of the van. He landed hard. Katie and Jacob didn't notice. They were looking at the dog. Aunt Kathleen and Aunt Mary didn't notice that Benjamin had fallen out of the van. They walked over to the man who was walking his dog.

"We're out of gas," Aunt Kathleen said to the man. "Can you help us?"

"I live over there," the man said. He pointed to a house near the gas station. "I have gas in a can in the back of my truck. I can get it for you. I'll be glad to help you." The man was indeed a kind man. His dog ran over to the van where Benjamin lay on the ground. The man didn't notice.

It was very dark now. Aunt Mary took out a small flashlight from her pocket. She shone it on the man.

"We'll wait here," Aunt Mary said.

Benjamin the Monkey lay sprawled on the hard ground beside the van. The dog sniffed at Benjamin's Esso hat. He licked at Benjamin's little white beard. He picked Benjamin up in his big soft mouth. He padded away. Benjamin screamed and screamed but no one heard him. He was only a stuffed animal.

Aunt Mary and Aunt Kathleen got back in the van that said Twinkle, Twinkle, Aerostar on the front. They didn't notice Benjamin was gone. The man came back with a can of gas. He emptied the gas into Rumblechum's gas tank. Aunt Mary and Aunt Kathleen thanked the man, jumped back into Rumblechum, and drove away.

Chapter 4

The Chase

The man stood in the dark. He looked at his truck, whistled for his dog and turned on the headlights in his truck. The big dog came running up to the man.

The dog had Benjamin in his big soft mouth.

"Please don't eat me, big dog," Benjamin said. "I'm made of cloth. I wouldn't taste good."

"I think you would taste like a bone." The dog growled and walked away from the man. "A big juicy bone."

"I wouldn't taste like a bone," Benjamin said. "I'd make you cough."

"You are soft, little monkey. You're right. You aren't like a bone."

"So spit me out. I'm not good to eat."

The man came closer to the dog.

"It's time to go home, Bailey," he said. Then the man looked closer at the dog.

"You have a stuffed monkey in your mouth! Where did you get that handsome monkey, Bailey?"

The dog growled. Benjamin was locked in Bailey's jaws. The man commanded Bailey to drop the stuffed monkey.

Benjamin fell out of the dog's mouth and onto the man's foot.

"You are a handsome monkey," the man said as he picked up Benjamin. "Did I see you before?"

"Yes," Benjamin said. "My two old friends and the children left me behind."

The man didn't hear him. Benjamin was only a stuffed monkey.

Benjamin wondered, if this was a dream? If it is a dream, where is Freedom? Freedom would not do this to me. What a bad dog. He was going to chew me to pieces. Can I trust this man? Oh, I miss Katie and Jacob and my friends! What will happen to me now?

As the man held Benjamin in his big hands, the buttons on Benjamin's coat twinkled in the headlights of the truck. The headlights also shone on Bailey. The man looked closely at Benjamin. He looked at Benjamin's hat that said "Esso" on it. He felt Benjamin's beard. Then he clapped one hand to his head.

"I know!" he said. "I bet you belong to the family who ran out of gas. How did you fall out of the van? Bailey must have found you when the door was open. The two ladies and the children have driven away. We will find them."

The man put Benjamin inside his truck. The big dog looked at Benjamin. He smiled, showing a lot of big white teeth.

"You're lucky I didn't swallow you. You're lucky you don't taste good."

"Nyah-nyah. I don't like this adventure. You're a bad dog. I miss Freedom and the children, Aunt Kathleen and Aunt Mary. We'll find them soon. I don't like a big dog. I don't like a very dark night. I don't like a gas station that's closed. I hope I never fall out of the van again."

The man said, "Get in the back, Bailey."

The dog jumped into the back of the man's truck. The man got into the cab beside Benjamin. He placed Benjamin on the dash. Then he started the truck.

"We'll find your friends," he said. They set off down the road after Rumblechum the van.

"They didn't miss me," Benjamin said. "What will I do if we don't find Rumblechum?"

The truck's headlights cut through the dark. They went past houses with yellow lights in their windows. They went past dark streets. They went past the limits of the town. They were trying to find Benjamin's family. Then they were back on the highway. The old truck was slow. Bailey the dog barked in the back. The man whistled to himself. The man drove carefully. They passed a car. They passed a Jeep. Then they saw the yellow headlights of a van in front of them. It was coming toward the truck on the other side of the road.

Benjamin was very excited. It was Rumblechum! The two aunts sat in the front seat. Jacob and Katie looked out the back window. Katie was crying. Jacob looked sad and anxious.

Then the children looked at the truck.

The van slowed down. The truck slowed down. Then they both stopped on opposite sides of the road. The man got out of the truck. He took a leash out of the back of the cab. He tied the leash to the dog's collar.

"There," he said. "That's better."

He took Benjamin out of the cab of the truck. Benjamin's buttons shone in the headlights of the van. His beard was dusty.

"Oh, Benjamin." Aunt Kathleen and Aunt Mary looked both ways and crossed the road. Katie and Jacob stayed in the van where it was safe. Katie wiped her eyes. She had stopped crying when she saw Benjamin again. She smiled. Jacob smiled, too.

"I knew we'd find him," Jacob said. He took off his glasses and wiped them on his sleeve.

"We didn't really think we'd see him again," Katie said.

"Did so," Jacob said, and that ended it. They yawned. It was very late. But they were both very glad to see Benjamin again.

"Is this your stuffed monkey?" asked the man. "He has many buttons on his coat. The buttons are from many different countries. He must have gone with you on lots of adventures. You must love him very much."

"Oh, Benjamin." Aunt Mary held Benjamin in her arms. "We were looking everywhere for you. We thought we'd lost you."

"Thank you, sir," Aunt Kathleen said to the man. She patted the dog's head. "Where did you find our stuffed monkey?"

"My dog had him in his mouth," the man said. "I'm sorry he took your monkey. Bailey should be on a leash. But it's a small town and late at night, so I thought it would be okay to let my dog run."

"Please keep him on a leash," Aunt Kathleen said. "He's a big dog. I'm glad he didn't hurt Benjamin."

"Thank you very much for rescuing me."

The man looked surprised. "Did you hear something?" he asked.

"Only the wind." Aunt Mary winked.

"Well, we should go now. We must find a gas station that's open, as that can of gas you gave us won't last long."

"There's a gas station and a motel a few miles down the road," the man said. "It's open all night. You can buy tea there, too, if you would like a cup. And milk and sandwiches for the children."

"Thank you again, sir," Aunt Kathleen said. "You're very kind. We're so glad to find Benjamin." She leaned over. She kissed Benjamin's soft cloth head.

Benjamin looked at the dog. The dog looked at Benjamin. The dog smiled and showed his big white teeth. Benjamin huddled in Aunt Mary's soft, warm arms.

Benjamin and the two aunts got back into the Aerostar.

"Oh, Benjamin."

Katie brushed a few strands of limp red hair from her forehead and wiped her eyes. She took Benjamin from Aunt Mary. She cradled him in her arms.

Jacob patted the little stuffed monkey on the head. "Good to see you, old chap," he said.

Aunt Kathleen turned Rumblechum around. They drove back down the highway, going east.

Chapter 5

A Good Night's Sleep

Rumblechum filled up with gas at the gas station that was open all night. When the aunts got out of the van they were careful to lock the doors so Benjamin wouldn't fall out again. The aunts put Benjamin on the dash so he could watch them. Aunt Mary woke up Jacob and Katie, who were sleeping in the back seat with their seatbelts fastened. Aunt Kathleen bought ham and cheese sandwiches to eat and chocolate milk to drink. Then they went to a motel for the night. They took Benjamin out of the van.

Benjamin slept with Katie in a big soft bed in one room of the motel. Jacob had a cot in the corner. He liked that. He pretended he was camping.

Benjamin dreamed about Freedom. He dreamed about Comfort, the stuffed Bear, and the wooly Lamb with the Red Cloth Heart, and the Puffin. He hoped their friends Della and Emily were taking good care of Freedom, the stuffed animals, and the old grey house with such a beautiful garden. Benjamin also dreamed about Bailey the Dog. He laughed in his dream.

"Ha, ha," he whispered, snug and warm in Katie's bed. "I got away. Dogs drool and monkeys rule." Benjamin giggled and wished Freedom could see how brave he was.

Aunt Mary stirred. "What did you say, Kathleen?" she said.

Aunt Kathleen was asleep in the bed next to Aunt Mary. Jacob snored softly from his cot. He had one arm thrown over his head. Katie smiled to herself. She heard Benjamin talk sometimes. No one else heard Benjamin talk. It felt like a whisper in her mind. You had to really love stuffed animals to hear them talk.

Outside their motel room, under the bright starlight, Rumblechum hissed and settled down for the night with creaks and groans. The van was full of gas. Aunt Kathleen had locked all the doors. Rumblechum was happy.

Benjamin saw a little mouse in the corner of the motel room.

"Good night, little mouse," he whispered.

He closed his eyes. He slept. The little mouse crept under the door and went into the night. Rumblechum saw him go.

"Good night, little mouse," and then all was quiet.

Katie smiled again in her sleep.

Chapter 6

Freedom's Dream

Della and Emily went every day into the old grey house while the children and their aunts were gone. They fed Freedom and filled her water dish. Emily played with Freedom and with all the stuffed animals. Emily loved stuffed animals, but she especially loved real calico cats like Freedom. Della loved Freedom, too. Freedom purred when Della and Emily stroked her.

Emily had a stuffed Kangaroo all the way from Australia which she called Wally the Roo. A friend from Down Under had brought it back for her after a visit. But she loved real critters better. She hugged Freedom and wished Freedom were her cat. She loved kittens, too, who grew up to be cuddly and warm and pur-r-r-y like Freedom. Emily missed Katie and Jacob very much, but she loved to look after Freedom when they were gone. Della knew that Emily was old enough to look after the children's calico cat. She had proven that by looking after Freedom so well so far.

Freedom missed Katie, Jacob, and the two aunts very much. She missed Benjamin, too. Benjamin had gone on an adventure. Benjamin already had so many adventures. But Freedom didn't have adventures. So Freedom slept and dreamed. She dreamed about the children and their aunts, who had driven off in Rumblechum to a place called O-N-T-A-R-I-O.

But mostly Freedom dreamed about Benjamin the Stuffed Monkey. Benjamin cuddled next to Freedom in her dreams. Benjamin talked to Freedom the Calico Cat in her dreams.

Benjamin whispered into Freedom's orange and white ear, "I love you, Freedom. I miss you. I'll tell you my adventures. I'll show you some tricks."

"I love you, too." Freedom tossed in her sleep. "Show me some tricks."

Benjamin romped and danced in Freedom's dreams. Benjamin threw his Esso cap into the air. He leapt onto a table and caught it again. He capered and pranced. Then he jumped onto Freedom and woke her up.

Benjamin was *not there*. Freedom was so disappointed. It was just a dream. Freedom looked around for another friend.

There was Comfort, the stuffed bear, sitting on the table where Katie had left him.

I remember the bear, Freedom said to herself, and looked past Comfort at the wooly stuffed animal who held a large red cloth heart.

"Do you remember a Kangaroo? Emily talks about Wally the Roo. Have you met Wally the Roo?"

"No, I'm a stuffed lamb and can't go out of this house. Ba-a-a-a. My mother was a sheep. See my soft woolly fleece?"

"Why are you holding a heart that says, 'I love you'?" Freedom had learned how to read without anyone knowing it. "Should I beware the heart?"

"Do not beware the heart," the lamb said. "I'm holding a Valentine heart. Someone who loved Katie very much gave it to her. Don't beware the bear. Comfort is a good bear. Someone who loved Aunt Kathleen gave him to her. And Aunt Kathleen gave him to Katie. Benjamin is a naughty monkey. He likes to tease. Don't believe everything Benjamin says."

"I want to talk to the Puffin," Freedom said. "I should remember the Puffin."

"The Puffin is from New Zealand," the wooly Stuffed Lamb said. "He is sitting on the table, too, as always."

Freedom stared. Sure enough, the stuffed black, white, and orange Puffin was perched on the table next to Comfort the Bear. They were souvenirs of Aunt Kathleen's trip to New Zealand. She'd brought back the toys for her niece.

"Beware the Puffin?"

"Not I," the small Puffin said. "Don't be afraid of me. Anyway, I'm not real. I'm a stuffed bird. Comfort the Bear and the Stuffed Lamb and Benjamin the Monkey are not real, either. We're all stuffed animals. But you're real, Freedom."

"Maybe Benjamin will be real one day, too."

"Maybe if he's very good. But I don't think he will be."

"No," Freedom said. "But Benjamin has gone on a great adventure with Katie and Jacob. They left me behind. They said I wouldn't like to travel so far."

"But you would?" Comfort the Bear wiped his nose with one brown paw.

"I would." Freedom hung her head.

"Poor Freedom," the Lamb said. "I hope they come back soon."

"Benjamin likes to travel," Freedom said. "I'd like to travel, too."

Freedom sighed and went back to sleep on Katie's little white bed. The lights next door glowed through the window.

Chapter 7

The Museum

The next day Aunt Mary, Aunt Kathleen, and the children drove across the border from Saskatchewan to the province of Manitoba. They passed many bright yellow fields of sunflowers and brilliant blue fields of flax. There are many farms in Manitoba. It also is very flat. They drove through the Red River Valley, where many settlers had come in the early days with their families in Red River carts drawn by oxen across the prairies. As they drove along, Aunt Mary and Aunt Kathleen talked about the early settlement of Manitoba, and the men and women and children who had journeyed across the prairies in huge creaking Red River carts behind plodding oxen. This intrigued Jacob.

"Tell me more." Jacob thought that would be such a great adventure.

They stopped at a museum. Jacob asked a lot of questions. He looked at all the exhibits. He studied the First Nations' artifacts, the utensils used by the settlers, the replicas of their cabins, and their clothing. He went into a tipi and saw the little drums, or tom-toms, the beaded jackets, the clay cooking pots and the arrowheads used by the First Nations people who were there when the white settlers first arrived in Manitoba. He saw a big replica of a Red River cart and many pictures of the men, women and children from faraway locations who had been drawn by oxen in these huge carts to build settlements in Manitoba.

Jacob and Katie looked and looked. Museums are very interesting places. Benjamin was interested. Katie took Benjamin with her into the room that looked like an old-fashioned schoolhouse. She propped Benjamin up at a very small oak desk with an inkwell on it. The inkwell was where the students had kept their bottles of black India ink. They dipped their quill pens into the India ink and wrote on lined paper under the teacher's direction. They copied letters from a book. They called it "penmanship." Katie knew how to write very well. She had good handwriting. She went up to the blackboard, took a piece of fat white chalk, and made a large "B" for Benjamin. She smiled at Benjamin.

"Time to go, children." Aunt Mary walked into the schoolroom. The yellow daisy bobbed on the side of her floppy hat. Jacob was behind her. He sucked on some rock candy he'd bought in the old-fashioned gift shop behind the museum.

"Want some, Katie?" Jacob held out a fistful of rock candy.

Aunt Kathleen smiled as Katie took one. They stopped to buy postcards before they left. Aunt Mary bought a pair of socks with frogs knitted on them.

Chapter 8

A Real Cowboy

They drove on to Brandon, Manitoba, which is west of Winnipeg on the Assiniboine River. The Trans-Canada Highway goes through Brandon. On the outskirts of Brandon they saw a sign that read "Rodeo today!"

"Oh, look, Mary," Aunt Kathleen said. "A rodeo! Let's go to the rodeo. We have never been to a real rodeo! It will be such fun. Let's go there, children."

And they did. Katie carried Benjamin in her backpack snug and warm, with his head and arms sticking out. They were anxious to see and learn all they could.

"What event should we watch first?" Aunt Mary patted Benjamin's head. The rodeo was very dusty. Many people wore big cowboy hats, drank pop, and ate hotdogs. Aunt Kathleen, Aunt Mary, the children, and Benjamin made their way through the rodeo grounds. They saw many events listed at different times and in different places. They were not yet sure which event they would attend.

Just then a tall, lanky cowboy ambled up to them from behind.

"That's a mighty fine looking monkey you've got there. Why, he's as cute as a kitten. I've always had a soft spot in my heart for them kind of stuffed animals," the cowboy said.

Aunt Kathleen stopped and turned around. "I took a fancy to him when I saw him at an Esso gas station in England." She smiled. "He just wiggled into my heart. We have traveled together to lots of far and near places. Now my niece has him."

"My name is Slim," the cowboy said, lifting his Stetson hat with one big brown hand. "What is your name, ma'am? Does the monkey have a name?"

"My name is Kathleen," Aunt Kathleen said. "This is my sister Mary. These children are Katie and Jacob. And this is Benjamin the Monkey."

"Fine rodeo you have here," Aunt Mary said. "Are you a real cowboy? Do you ride a horse?"

"I surely do." Slim the Cowboy looked down at his cowboy boots and hitched up his jeans. "What do you all know about the rodeo?"

"Why, we've never been to a rodeo," Aunt Mary said. "This is a new adventure for us. It's the first rodeo for Katie and Jacob, too."

"Mighty fine day for your first rodeo," the cowboy said, and smiled at the children. "This being your first rodeo, let me tell you a bit about it. There are five main events. There's saddle bronc riding, where cowboys like old Slim here ride a bucking bronc. A *bronc* is a horse that bucks or jumps. It tries to throw the rider off."

"Oh." Katie sucked in her breath from where she stood waist-high to the cowboy. "I wouldn't like that. The horse looks very big and mean."

Jacob was also very interested. "I think that's *cool*," Jacob said. "*I* wouldn't be afraid, Slim."

"'Course not," Slim said. "Then there's bareback bronc riding, where cowboys ride a bucking horse without a saddle."

"That would be difficult," Aunt Kathleen said.

"There's bull riding, where cowboys try to ride a large bucking bull with their hands locked into a rope tied around the bull's middle. The bulls are big and mean and mad."

"*Yes.*" Benjamin squeaked with excitement. Nobody heard him.

"There's steer wrestling, or bulldogging, where a cowboy on a horse runs after a steer. Then the cowboy gets off his horse and tries to throw the steer to the ground."

"Poor steer," Aunt Mary said.

Poor cowboy, Benjamin thought. He could get thrown, or even stomped on.

"There's calf roping, too, where the cowboy shows off his skill with a lasso, or looped rope, by roping a calf."

Jacob wondered if he could do that.

"There's also barrel racing, where cowgirls ride their horses around a course of barrels. They get a penalty if they knock over a barrel."

"The winner is the cowgirl who completes the event in the fastest time."

"How exciting!" Aunt Kathleen said.

Aunt Mary looked at the children. "What should we watch first?"

"Well, I'd like to invite you to the saddle bronc riding coming right up," the cowboy said.

"What is your favorite event, Slim?" Aunt Kathleen said.

"Saddle bronc riding is my favorite. I'm going to ride a bronc, or bucking horse, coming up shortly." Then the cowboy stammered a bit and scuffed one boot into the dust. He looked at Benjamin. Then he looked at Katie.

"Little girl, I don't mean to offend," the cowboy said. "But I really would be much obliged if—that is, well—can I take Benjamin with me on the ride? Sure would be obliged. I'd be very careful with him. He'd be kind of like a good luck monkey to me. Always had a soft spot in my heart for little critters like him."

The cowboy tugged at the brim of his big hat and rubbed his chin.

Aunt Kathleen and Aunt Mary looked at each other. Then they smiled. They looked at Katie. Katie smiled and nodded. Aunt Mary took Benjamin out of Katie's backpack and handed Benjamin to the cowboy. Slim tucked Benjamin carefully into his shirt. He threw one long leg over the fence and ambled up to the chute. A big black horse was in the chute, snorting and bucking. Slim climbed up on the side of the chute and waited for his name to be called. Excited, Jacob and Katie walked over to the fence and leaned between the bars to watch. Their aunts leaned over the fence and watched, too.

Chapter 9

A Bucking Bronc

Benjamin could not believe what was happening to him. He peered out of Slim's shirt at the horse bucking around in the small chute below him. Benjamin felt the tension in the air.

He hoped he wouldn't get jostled out of the cowboy's shirt and stomped on. But he drew a deep breath and thought brave thoughts.

"Slim Johnston riding *Killer*," the loudspeaker said.

Slim lowered himself onto the bucking bronc. Then the chute opened and out they went. The horse bucked and twisted into the air. The cowboy hung on tightly to the rope with one hand. He waved his other hand into the air for balance. Benjamin was very scared. He was also very excited. He had never done anything like this before. Dust flew all around.

"What a ride!" The loudspeaker blared. "That's Slim Johnston on Killer, folks! Looks like Slim's going to stay on that bronc!"

Around and around the ring they went, Killer twisting and bucking for all he was worth. Slim was almost hidden by a cloud of dust. Then a whistle blew and the cowboy jumped to the ground. Benjamin had been jostled almost out of the cowboy's shirt. He was safe—a little dusty but still very much intact. What a ride it had been!

On the sidelines again, the cowboy patted Benjamin's soft cloth head. "How you doing, little buddy?"

"I wish Freedom the Calico Cat could see me now," Benjamin said to Slim, looking up at the dusty face of the cowboy.

"What's that, little buddy?" Slim said with surprise and leaned down to look at Benjamin. "You're talking to me, little friend. Well, that shouldn't surprise old Slim. And I'm not surprised to find out those two nice little children have a calico cat at home. They're just the type to have lots of love for stuffed animals and calico cats."

"I miss Freedom." Benjamin sighed. "I wish you could meet her, Slim."

"Well, maybe I will someday," Slim said. "I've traveled a lot myself, little buddy. I've been in rodeos all over the world."

His boots scuffed in the dirt as he walked to the side of the corral near the man with the loudspeaker.

"My horses and I have been in the Calgary Stampede many times. I've also been in the United States, in Cheyenne, Wyoming; in Las Vegas, Nevada; in Denver, Colorado; in Houston, Texas. I've even been to Mexico and Spain."

Benjamin was now snug again in the cowboy's shirt. Slim patted the little stuffed monkey on the head.

"We've much in common, Benjamin. We've both traveled and had adventures. I wish I could take you with me, but that couldn't be. Katie would miss you too much."

"I live in Edmonton, Alberta," Benjamin said. "Aunt Kathleen and Aunt Mary can give you our address. Maybe you can visit us there one day."

"Mighty fine idea," the cowboy said.

The loudspeaker called his name again. The last event of the day was over.

"The winner of the saddle bronc riding contest is *Slim Johnston*," the man at the loudspeaker said. He was standing in the arena.

"Come on over here, Slim."

Slim had won the saddle bronc riding contest with Benjamin today! He ambled up to the microphone and took the big belt buckle he had won.

"I owe it all to my little buddy, Benjamin."

Slim pulled the stuffed monkey out of the front of his shirt and held him high. The other cowboy at the microphone smiled and gave Benjamin a rodeo pin from a box. He pinned it on Benjamin's Esso coat. Benjamin was very proud. The cowboy's friends surrounded him and pounded him on the back. The new rodeo pin on Benjamin's coat shone brightly in the warm Manitoba sun. Then the cowboy ambled up to Aunt Mary and Aunt Kathleen. He carried the big belt buckle he had won. He handed Benjamin back to Katie.

"Mighty fine ride, Slim," the aunts said. "We are so proud of you, Benjamin!" They carefully put Benjamin back into Katie's backpack.

"Where to now, ladies?" Slim said.

"We're going to Winnipeg," Aunt Mary and Aunt Kathleen said together. "We're going to the Royal Winnipeg Ballet tonight with Benjamin and the children."

"Don't suppose I could have your address back home, ladies?" Slim said and scuffed his boot in the dust. "Got something in mind to send to my little pal here."

Won't Freedom be surprised? Benjamin thought with excitement. What could it be?

"We'd be happy to give you our address, Slim," the aunts said, walking back to Rumblechum with their arms around the lanky cowboy. "And where might we find you, to thank you again?"

"I travel with the rodeo," Slim said. "I go south in the winter and I'm up here in the summer. I'm a traveling man, ma'am, but I reckon I could give you my sister's address here in Winnipeg. You could get in touch with me through her."

Katie and Jacob buckled themselves into their seats in the back of the van. The aunts placed Benjamin on the dash again so he could see the cowboy from the side window.

"It's been a real pleasure," Slim said. "'Bye, children. 'Bye, Benjamin."

He winked and waved as they drove away. Rumblechum went Rumblechum, Rumbelchum, Rum, Rum, Rum.

Benjamin watched the cowboy turn and walk away, back to the rodeo, where a few minutes before Benjamin had bounced and jostled about with the cowboy on the back of a bucking bronc!

Chapter 10

Freedom's Adventure

Aunt Kathleen and Aunt Mary had always lived together in the old, two-story house in Edmonton, with the sagging fence and beautiful garden. Before the children came, there had just been the stuffed animals, including Benjamin the Stuffed Monkey and Freedom the real calico cat with them. That seemed to be enough.

"But there's always room for two more!" Aunt Kathleen said when she heard about the children, slapping her floppy hat onto her head sideways so the flower fell over her eyes.

"Yes!" Aunt Mary said. She tugged at her pearls and rolled up the sleeves of her old red sweater. So the children came to stay. Freedom remembered that day, now that she was alone in the house, waiting for someone to come and play with her and give her food and water. Every day Della and sometimes her daughter Emily visited the fluffy calico cat; sometimes more than once a day.

The house had hardwood floors and many little rooms. Outside, a crooked gate hung by its hinges. A fence sagged around a yard strewn with raspberries and wild flowers, and a real wishing well. A mailbox with painted frogs stood beside the crooked gate.

Emily skipped through the sagging gate this particular Saturday morning, back door key in her hand. Her mother Della trusted her to open the old creaking back door and give Freedom fresh water and food, and play with Freedom for half an hour or more every Saturday morning and often after school. Emily was daydreaming as she turned the key in the lock. The sun was shining warmly and she could smell the fresh scent of flowering shrubs from the backyard next to the door. Oh! Oh! She left the door open when she went into the house.

Freedom came galumph galumph down the rickety old stairs into the kitchen when she heard Emily come in. Freedom loved to eat the treats that Della left on the counter for Emily to give her. Freedom gobbled down the moist food Emily put in her dish and looked around for more. The sunlight streamed through the little window that overlooked the back yard. Emily stroked Freedom's soft fur. Then she skipped into the living room and began to play with a beautiful porcelain doll that sat on top of Aunt Mary's piano. She forgot about Freedom.

Freedom looked up at the window. She would love to go out into that bright sunshine. Then she sniffed the air. She smelled fresh air coming from the open door. A little breeze brought the scent of roses and wildflowers to her sensitive nose. Freedom walked towards the open door, looking back over her furry shoulders at Emily. Emily was playing with the doll out of sight in the living room. Freedom stood in the open doorway, uncertain whether to go farther. She sniffed the air. She looked around. Finally she ventured outside.

An uneven concrete path led to the tangled backyard. There were shrubs and trees in the back yard as well as a vegetable garden. A big spruce tree spread its dark branches by the garage. A sundial stood in one corner by the old brown deck. Robins sang and jays cackled. Freedom strolled into the vegetable garden and rolled in the warm black earth. She closed her big yellow eyes and puffs of dust rose around her as she stretched in the sunlight. A dogwood bush was in flower at the corner of the little garden. Sweet scents filled the air.

Now there were baby birds in the magpies' nest in the big spruce tree on the corner. The baby magpies were just learning to fly. One had hopped and flapped its way onto the ground beneath the tree. And the mother and father magpies thought, *Oh, Oh – Cat! Oh, Oh Cat! Cats eat baby birds!* And they started to cackle and rose from the branches on which they were perched. They swung about Freedom's head, dive bombing like little planes in war, pecking at Freedom's head, cawing and making such a noise! Over and over again the black and white birds attacked the puzzled cat who was sprawled in the dust, enjoying the sun, eyes half closed, wondering what the ruckus was about. Poor innocent Freedom, who wouldn't hurt a bird. She leapt to her feet and shook her head. The birds cawed and circled her, aiming for her big yellow eyes, screeching *Cat! Cat! Go away!*

Freedom looked over at the baby bird, who could not spread its wings enough to fly back into the nest. The baby bird was hopping around the ground, and the mother and father birds were rat-tat-tatting like machine guns and diving at Freedom's head. Freedom thought, I wouldn't hurt the baby bird. She didn't know what to do. She tried to get out of the garden but the birds kept swooping past her head, driving her away from the tree. The breeze had picked up, and Freedom's fur was ruffled and full of dirt from her dust bath in the garden. She felt confused and very frightened.

Just then Emily realized that she had left Freedom alone. She came running out of the living room and into the kitchen. She saw the open door and heard the ruckus in the garden. Her heart beat wildly. She picked up a large wooden spoon from the jar on the counter. What was making that awful noise? Was Freedom all right? Oh, her mother would be so cross that she had left Freedom alone with an open door. Now she would never be allowed to have the key again. Her mother would never trust her, and the aunts and Katie and Jacob would be so disappointed in her.

"Oh, Freedom!" Emily cried, running into the garden. Freedom opened her eyes wide and ran towards Emily in great bounding leaps. Emily yelled and waved the wooden spoon at the screeching birds and they flew back into their tree. The baby bird in the meantime had managed to flap onto a low branch. The birds sat in the tree and preened their blue black feathers. They looked very satisfied with themselves. They were quiet once again. A chickadee trilled from somewhere. The wind stirred the branches of the dogwood but Freedom was not interested in the scents of the garden anymore. She snuggled into Emily's arms and allowed herself to be carried back into the house.

Oh, thought Freedom, that was enough adventure for me! I don't want any more adventures, thank you. And she didn't venture into the garden again that summer, nor did she roll in the dust and bask in the warmth of the yellow sun gilding the roses outside, although cats love to do that. She stayed in the old house and waited for the aunts and the children to come home again, and thought of Benjamin, and didn't long for another adventure of her own until—well, until next year. But that's another story.

And Della, in her starched apron, said to Emily, "Everyone makes mistakes, dear. Just be more careful next Saturday. After all, you rescued dear Freedom from the parent birds, who were protecting their baby. Have some cookies and milk. After all, you've had a little adventure, too!"

Chapter 11

Love

Off Aunt Kathleen, Aunt Mary and the children went to Winnipeg, the capital city of Manitoba and the oldest city in the Prairie Provinces. Benjamin was sad to leave the cowboy, but he could hardly wait to watch his first ballet that night. It was the first ballet for Jacob and Katie, too.

They watched the performance of *Beauty and the Beast* by the Royal Winnipeg Ballet. They had good seats in the second row. Benjamin was fascinated with Belle as she leapt about the stage in her spangled costume. He felt tired after such an exciting day, and thought often of the cowboy, but was enchanted with Belle. He felt himself falling in love with her. She was beautiful. And so graceful. The ballerina looked down at him once, right in the face, and Benjamin felt his little cloth heart stop and then beat kerchunk, kerchunk. Oh, Belle was a beauty! No wonder the Beast had fallen in love with her. He glanced over at the children. He thought Jacob was in love with Belle, too.

They spent intermission looking down into the orchestra pit. There were violins, trumpets, stringed instruments, tubas and French horns, drums, and a big golden harp. The musicians tuned their instruments.

Jacob liked the percussion instruments the best. The drummer was chubby and had a beard, like Benjamin. The drummer's beard was big and black. He wore a tuxedo and banged on his cymbals and pounded on the big bass drums and the smaller kettledrums and even shook the tambourines. Jacob wanted to be a drummer, too. But most of all he wanted to meet Belle.

And so did Benjamin. How Benjamin wished he were real!

Benjamin snuggled into Katie's pocket after the performance. He didn't meet Belle. But ever after that night he would hold a little part of Belle in his heart, soft and melting. Like the Beast, who also fell in love with her. That night Benjamin dreamed he was real and dancing with Belle. He dreamed he was with Freedom, and all the stuffed animals at home were real. They all went on a real adventure together. He snuggled up to Katie where he slept and whimpered a little in his sleep.

* * *

A week later, back home in Alberta, a parcel arrived at Freedom's door addressed to Benjamin. Emily was sitting on the front step sipping a glass of lemonade. Della was playing the piano while Freedom sprawled at her feet. Emily took the package from the mailman and gave it to her mother.

"What is this?" Della said. "A parcel for Benjamin? Whatever could it be?"

"He must have had an adventure." Emily raised her eyebrows. "Someone has sent him a parcel."

Freedom was very curious about what was in the package. But she was happy Benjamin got some mail. Maybe it meant her beloved friends would be home soon. Della took the package and laid it on the dining room table.

"Maybe they'll be home soon," she said.

Freedom smiled as a cat smiles, to herself. She purred as she climbed the stairs and jumped up on Katie's bed, with Comfort the Bear and the Stuffed Lamb with a Heart, and the other stuffed animals around her where Emily had placed them. She curled up and waited. She waited for Aunt Mary and Aunt Kathleen and Katie and Jacob to come home. She thought about Benjamin.

She wondered what was in the parcel. Hope was rising. They would be home soon. Something in the parcel had jangled when Della put it down. What could it be? Freedom continued to purr, thinking of Katie and Jacob. And thinking of Benjamin. Freedom no longer wished she could have an adventure, too. But someone had to stay home to look after things, she thought, and looked at Della and Emily with large yellow loving eyes.

Chapter 12

Ontario at Last

At last they arrived in Ontario. It is a huge province. The aunts, the children, and Benjamin had traveled and traveled, yet they were still in Ontario, unlike Alberta, Saskatchewan and Manitoba, which they had traveled through in a day.

Ontario was a beautiful province. Maple trees grew everywhere, as well as a variety of conifer trees, ones bearing needles. It was mid-summer, and the maple trees swayed in a brisk west wind.

"Look, children," Aunt Mary said. "How the leaves are fresh and green, and glisten in the sun."

Aunt Kathleen said, "In the fall, the maple trees will have splendid leaves of red and gold and brown that swirl to the grey sky. Then they will drop, one by one, or all in a flurry, to the still-green grass or dark soil about their roots."

Benjamin looked out from his position on Rumblechum's dash, where Katie had placed him, as he had a better vantage point from there.

"Here in the winter, a wet snow falls, unlike Alberta's drier snow. The roads here get very icy. Everything freezes. People ice skate on the Rideau Canal in Ottawa for fourteen miles. Ottawa is the capital of Canada," Aunt Kathleen said. "We won't see Ottawa, or Eastern Ontario, where the sugar maples are. We have no time to go there this trip. Maybe another time."

"This time it's central Ontario for us," Katie said. "And I'm hoping there won't be any ice for months."

"I can't imagine ice and snow on this wonderful hot, sunny day," Aunt Mary said.

"There was an ice storm in 1998 across Eastern Ontario that sent maple tree sugar bush branches crashing to the ground," Aunt Kathleen said. "It affected the crop for years."

"Maple sugaring time is in March and April," Aunt Mary said. "When plastic tubes are put into the forest of sugar maple trees or sugar bushes, and the sweet sap is drawn off to large evaporator containers in a sugar camp, and boiled down. There are country restaurants with benches and big tables where you can eat eggs fried in maple syrup, and maple syrup in your coffee, and sausages made with maple syrup, and pancakes with maple syrup, and maple syrup on toast."

"There is a Maple Festival in Perth, Ontario, every year at that time. It's more fun than a rodeo." Aunt Kathleen laughed.

"Yummy," Jacob said.

It sounded very delicious and interesting. He would like to travel to Eastern Ontario in the springtime. But he didn't like ice and snow. He was glad it was summer now. Summer in Ontario was beautiful. So beautiful and historic, too.

"Beautiful except for the mosquitoes," Katie said.

And the black flies. The four travelers drove some more. Ontario was rugged and big. Jacob forgot about spring-time and maple syrup as he looked ahead. There was so much scenery to enjoy. Aunt Mary, Aunt Kathleen, Katie, Benjamin, and he, were going to camp in this rugged, beautiful wilderness tonight. What fun! Jacob loved to camp. He rubbed his glasses with the sleeve of his shirt. His sturdy, red-haired sister loved to camp, too.

They finally found a nice campground by one of the lakes. Tall swaying trees stood all around. Jacob inhaled the sweet aroma of pine and spruce. And the birds! Wax-wings, cardinals, and bluebirds, robins and jays, all sang and darted through the fresh air. They sprang from the fluffy grey clouds overhead. Landing on the trees, they clung to the slim branches at the ends of the massive limbs with strong match-like brown feet.

Aunt Kathleen and Aunt Mary unloaded Rumblechum. Cooking supplies were put on a picnic table. Then they put up a tarp overhead in case it rained. They pitched the tent. Then they built a bonfire in the middle of the camp, and they roasted wieners and marshmallows. The sun went down. The stars came out. A pale wedge of the moon appeared. The clouds sailed away. They sang songs in the dark, while thousands of mosquitoes buzzed about. They swatted and snapped at the mosquitoes. There were little black flies, too. The children and the two aunts squirted insect spray from a bottle onto their arms and legs and hands and feet. They rubbed insect spray on their faces and ears and necks. They sang some more songs. The mosquitoes and flies didn't bother Benjamin.

Then they went to bed once again in the new dome tent they had bought just for this trip. This tent was bigger than their last tent. It also had a screen across the doorway. The mosquitoes and black flies didn't come in. The aunts tucked Benjamin into Katie's sleeping bag. Everyone had their own air mattress and sleeping bag. Then they went to sleep.

Chapter 13

A Truly Great Lake

In the early morning they could hear the lonesome sound of loons across the lake.

"Hear the loons, Katie?" Aunt Mary turned over in her sleeping bag.

Katie lay still and listened to the loons. She was eager to get up and travel again, as they still had a long way to go to get to Manitoulin Island. Soon Aunt Kathleen and Aunt Mary got up and made breakfast. They had sausages, pancakes, and orange juice from a bottle. The children gobbled their breakfast. They were still in their pajamas. Then they got dressed. The aunts packed up Rumblechum again and started off.

Jacob remembered the Red River Valley in which they had camped in Manitoba, and wondered if settlers had ever come here to Ontario. Men and women had certainly settled in northern Ontario with their families. The men were miners who mined copper, iron and nickel ore in underground mines. Here in northern Ontario there were lakes and vast forests.

"Too bad we don't fish," Aunt Kathleen said. "There are a lot of great fish to be caught in these lakes."

"Oh, could we sometime?" Jacob said. "I'd love to catch a big fish."

The four travelers and Benjamin traveled and traveled through the rugged and rocky Canadian Shield, and finally arrived at Thunder Bay on Lake Superior, the largest of the Great Lakes. Thunder Bay is the heart of the grain shipping area on the Great Lakes. Grain terminals were all along the side of the lake.

"Lake Superior looks so much smaller on a map than it is in reality," Aunt Mary said. "It'll take us a long time to drive around it."

They headed eastward and eventually arrived at *Wawa*, an Indian word for giant goose. A giant goose made from Algoma steel stands high on the cliff above the highway and beckons passersby to stop for awhile. Aunt Kathleen took a photograph of Katie and Jacob sitting on the base of the giant goose. They held Benjamin.

The travelers got to Marathon, close to the eastern side of Lake Superior. What a marathon it is to drive over the top end of Lake Superior. It's a very big lake. That's why it's called a Great Lake, Katie supposed.

Many hours later they arrived at Sault St. Marie right on the east side of Lake Superior.

"It won't be long now before we get to the Island," Aunt Kathleen said.

Oh goody, Jacob thought. He'd like to explore the island.

Chapter 14

Over The Swing Bridge and to Cousin Tom's

Finally they arrived at the Swing Bridge which connects Manitoulin Island to the mainland. Aunt Kathleen and Aunt Mary's cousin lived on the island. They had to stop because the bridge was swung open to allow the boat traffic through. Every hour on the hour it swings around, making way for the boats. While waiting for the bridge to swing back, Aunt Kathleen told Katie and Jacob that their Great Uncle Will used to pilot the ferry between the mainland and the island before the Swing Bridge was built.

Benjamin was sitting on the dashboard of the van, where he could see all the action. Rumblechum went Rumblechum, Rumblechum, Rum, Rum, Rum, over the Swing Bridge to the island on the other side. In less than an hour Aunt Mary and Aunt Kathleen drove across the island to Manitouwaning to their cousin Tom's house.

Tom saw them coming down the road towards his big old farmhouse.

"Oh, boy!" Tom said. "Visitors! They told me they were coming soon. I'll feed two hungry children and their aunts a mess of fish for supper, which I caught myself, and potatoes and peas from my garden. I hope they're hungry. I was feeling lonesome. It will be nice to visit with my cousins from Alberta. I hope they stay a long time. This big old farmhouse has lots of room."

Katie turned around in her seat and looked behind, for she was shy with strangers, and thought cousin Tom looked big and somewhat old to her, standing in his yard alone. Katie didn't know what lay ahead for them, on this holiday on Manitoulin Island with cousin Tom. Jacob, however, eagerly got out of the van when it stopped and ran up to cousin Tom, who stood with a fishing rod in his hands.

"Fish for supper," Tom said, and hugged Aunt Kathleen and Aunt Mary.

"Great!" Jacob said.

Katie brought up the rear. However, she noticed the smile wrinkles around Tom's eyes. He has a kind face, she thought. Like the man in Maryfield.

Tom, when he first saw Aunt Kathleen and Aunt Mary in Rumblechum, hit his head with his hand and said, "Oh, great! Here come those two lady cousins and—what's that critter sitting on the dash? Whatever will I do with a stuffed monkey?"

Tom lived all alone in a big old farmhouse. He didn't have a lot of company. But when he saw the children in the back seat he smiled. Tom really liked children. And he really liked the two aunts, too. He just *pretended* to like being alone.

The children saw through him, to the kind and somewhat lonely man at heart. They enjoyed the trout dinners, and the talks in the lingering twilight on the big front porch, where they swung to and fro on a bench suspended by chains.

Aunt Kathleen and Aunt Mary took over the cooking and cleaning tasks while they were there. Tom seemed content to let them do that. He sometimes brought them fish to fry, or frozen grouse to prepare. They often ate supper on the front porch, facing a pink and gold sunset over the rim of the island. Tom told them stories of the Island, and drew them maps of places they could visit. One day he told them about the Cup and Saucer. Then they decided to go there, as their first adventure on Manitoulin Island.

Chapter 15

The Cup and Saucer

The next day the children and their aunts went hiking on a trail Tom had told them about that led to a rocky place named the Cup and Saucer. Benjamin rode along in Katie's backpack, as usual. Aunt Mary and Aunt Kathleen had walking sticks and backpacks, too, and so did Jacob. They wore hiking shorts, long cotton stockings up to their knees, and sturdy hiking boots. There was unscented soap and towels to wipe their hands and faces when they got dirty, and there were water bottles; sandwiches, and apples to eat in their backpacks. And there was Benjamin.

"Huff, puff." Aunt Kathleen strode ahead of Aunt Mary up the Cup and Saucer, so named because of the curious rock formation that looked like a cup and saucer. They were very high up. Little rocks rattled from under their feet and down onto the Saucer. Benjamin was afraid to look down. Katie squeezed through rock crevices and clambered up the rocky cliffs behind Aunt Kathleen.

Suddenly, Katie stopped. She had just squeezed through another crevice. Her backpack was stuck. She pulled and pulled. Benjamin squeaked with fear.

Katie pulled and pulled on her backpack. Then it came free from the crevice in which it was stuck and she lurched forward. She grasped the root of a tree which was clinging to the side of the Cup. Aunt Mary gasped.

Benjamin was stuck in a rock crevice. He had been pulled out of the backpack! His little white beard trembled in the breeze that blew through the crevice. His Esso button shone in the sun. His two little hands protruded from the crevice. His little cloth body was stuck tight in the space between two rocks. Katie pulled on Benjamin's upper body, which was all she could see of her dear little cloth friend. His jacket and legs were stuck tight in the crevice. Benjamin could see far below, where a small stream trickled into the Cup like a ribbon of silver.

"Oh, woe is me," Benjamin said to the wind. "I'm stuck tight. If I'm pulled out I may fall and drown in the river of water I see far below. If I stay here the eagles might get me and tear me to shreds. The hawks might take my shiny buttons and the pin I won at the rodeo. The ravens might line their nests with the threads of my jacket. A rockslide might cover me."

"Don't worry, children," Aunt Kathleen said, from the other side of the crevice. "We'll get Benjamin out of that hole."

She tugged from the other side at Benjamin's stocking feet. "Really, Benjamin. We must get you some shoes."

"Don't talk of shoes at a time like this," Aunt Mary said, pushing on Benjamin's soft little head with the Esso cap and the buttons on it.

In the meantime, Aunt Kathleen continued to pull. "Oh," cried Benjamin. "You're pulling me apart!"

Chapter 16

Katie Has an Idea

"We are pulling him apart," Aunt Mary said, clinging to a root in the rock face. Far above, yellow flowers bloomed at the top of the Cup.

"I know," Katie said. "We'll make him wet and slippery. We have soap to wash our hands, and there's water in the water bottles in our backpacks. We'll lather him up and he will sli-i-i-de out."

Oh, no! thought Benjamin. I'm going to drown right here in this very rock crevice.

Katie and Aunt Kathleen lathered up Benjamin's jacket and legs that were sticking out on their side of the crevice. Aunt Mary pulled one more time from her side. She wasn't very gentle. Benjamin popped out of the crevice. Aunt Mary hugged him and kissed his little monkey face. She wiped and dried him off carefully with one of the towels. Katie carried Benjamin in her arms to the top of the Cup, where the yellow flowers bloomed, and she laid him in the sun to dry. In no time, the golden sun and the warm breeze dried the soap and water from Benjamin's jacket, legs, and little body.

"Oh, I wish Freedom could see me now," Benjamin said as he was placed once more in Katie's backpack for the trip back down. The sun was low in the west when they finally reached the bottom of the Saucer. What an adventure!

Chapter 17

A Fishy Story

The next day they went boating on Lake Mindemoya. Nothing happened to Benjamin that day, but he was very careful to stay in the middle of the boat. Tom rowed and rowed. Tom was a good fisherman. They caught a lot of fish. Jacob's dream of going fishing and even catching a big fish had come true. Jacob caught a big trout with Tom's old rod and reel. Just before they rowed home for a trout supper, there was an accident.

Tom wore a khaki sun hat in the boat when he fished. The sun hat was full of buttons and other things that fishermen wear on their hats. Jacob sat next to Tom and threaded a big juicy worm onto his hook. Then Jacob cast the fishing line out into the lake. The line arced backwards and then forwards, over Tom's head. The hook caught on Tom's hat as it whipped past his ear, and the hat landed in the middle of Lake Mindemoya. The hat didn't sink at first. Tom's hair blew in the wind.

"Oh, no!" Jacob said, as Tom's hat floated many yards from the boat. "I'm sorry, Tom. I'll reel your hat back into the boat."

That's what he did. When Tom got his hat back, it was all wet and sopping. Guess what? The little worm was crawling around on the brim, all wet and sopping, too.

Later that week, they visited more of Aunt Kathleen and Aunt Mary's relatives and also some friends of Tom. They bought honey, maple sugar candy, and sweaters to take home to their friends, especially Della and her daughter Emily, who were looking after Freedom and their house. They found a white stuffed smiling polar bear for Emily, and a video and wooden bird call for Della. They bought a toy for Freedom. They bought a new button for Benjamin. They bought a blanket for themselves with bright pictures of Manitoulin Island. The blanket said, "North Channel," "Mississagi Straits" and "Manitoulin Island" on it. There was a picture of a mill and other places of interest on it. They bought Jacob his very own fishing rod and a sun hat with matching socks for Katie.

Chapter 18

The Time Has Come, The Walrus Said…

They were very happy on the island. Tom had lots of good things for them to eat; there were fun places to see, and many friends and relatives to visit. But Katie was home-sick and missed Freedom the calico cat. She also missed Comfort, the stuffed Koala Bear, and the woolly stuffed Lamb with the large red cloth heart that said, "I love you." She missed the small black, white, and orange Puffin bird from New Zealand. She missed her friends, dear Della and Emily, too, who had stayed behind to care for the beloved old house and its occupants.

Jacob did not miss anybody. He was happy going fish-ing every day with Tom and climbing cliffs. His glasses were often dirty. Tom wore big dark sunglasses and he always wore his fishing hat.

One day, Aunt Mary rose from her bed in their cousin's spare room, stretched, yawned, and put on a robe. As she padded out to the front porch, she said to her sister and to Tom, "Well, hasn't this been great. You've shown us a good time, Tom. We love you. But it's time to go home now."

Aunt Kathleen agreed.

Hearing this made Jacob unhappy for a while, but then he thought about Freedom and home. They had been guests on Manitoulin Island for more than three weeks. He was not tired of fishing, but there were more adventures, he was sure, before they got home. Katie thought it was time to go home.

Tom had grown to love his two cousins and the children, too. He was sad to see them go. The children hugged Tom and promised to keep in touch.

Away they went in Rumblechum, down the road, across the Island, over the Swing Bridge, and back on the highway, headed west this time, instead of east. Home.

Chapter 19

Going Home

They drove and drove back across Ontario, stopping at Whitefish where the story of Winnie the Pooh originated, and at the Terry Fox Memorial just east of Thunder Bay. Katie and Jacob bought a Winnie the Pooh book and other souvenirs at Whitefish. They took photographs at the Winnie the Pooh sculpture. Terry Fox is a famous man with one leg who ran almost across Canada. Winnie the Pooh is a famous bear. Benjamin wondered if *he* would ever become famous. They took pictures of the Terry Fox Memorial. Then they went on.

They drove for days. Finally, they reached the border of Ontario. They drove across the prairies. Through Manitoba and Saskatchewan, past wheat and barley fields already turning golden, and bright yellow canola fields, which were being harvested. As Aunt Mary and Aunt Kathleen and the children traveled along, they entertained themselves. They ate apples and oranges, drank pineapple juice, and sang traveling songs. Benjamin sat on the dash of the van and looked out at all the flat fields and late summer colors. He remembered Slim the cowboy in Brandon, Manitoba. He remembered Bailey the dog and the kind man in Maryfield, Saskatchewan. He remembered beautiful Belle who danced before him at the Royal Winnipeg Ballet in Winnipeg. He remembered Tom on Manitoulin Island. He remembered all the adventures.

But most of all he thought about Freedom the calico cat, and the old grey two-story house with the sagging fence and the beautiful garden. The house where he lived with Aunt Kathleen, Aunt Mary, the children, and the stuffed animals, in Edmonton, Alberta. He hoped they would soon be back home. He was bursting with stories to tell.

Chapter 20

Home Sweet Home

At last they arrived back at the old grey house in Edmonton. Adventures were great. But it was better to be home.

And you know what?

Freedom was at the door, meowing with excitement and joy to see her beloved family.

Aunt Kathleen, Aunt Mary, and the children were overjoyed to see Freedom, too. They had presents for Freedom. A grey woolen mouse stuffed with catnip. A wind-up blue toy bird that skittered about the floor in front of Freedom, and treats to eat. Benjamin was very thrilled to be back home and see his old friend Freedom again.

Benjamin was very excited when he saw the package addressed to him. Katie opened it. There was a note inside from the cowboy. The package contained a wee pair of cowboy boots for Benjamin. And a new red collar with a tiny brass saddle on it for Freedom. There was a cowboy hat for Jacob and a dress with real fringes for Katie. The note said, Love, from your friend Slim.

Freedom was very happy with her new collar with the brass saddle. Benjamin whispered to her about how he had ridden a bucking bronc with a real cowboy, and had the pin to prove it. Katie carefully pulled the little cowboy boots onto Benjamin's stocking feet. They fit perfectly. Now he had shoes. Not just any shoes, either. He had cowboy boots just like Slim. Benjamin felt like a real cowboy. He snuggled next to Freedom. He loved to travel. But now he was glad to be home. He was glad to see Freedom again, and all his many other friends. He had so many tales of adventures to share with them.

But he often thought of the cowboy, and of Belle, and of Tom on Manitoulin Island, and the long drive home.

Katie and Jacob went back to school. The two aunts, the children, Benjamin, and Freedom continued to live together in the old house in Edmonton, Alberta. The children often talked about their wonderful trip through Alberta, Saskatchewan, Manitoba, and Ontario. They often talked long-distance on the telephone to their cousin, Tom on Manitoulin Island. And they told their friends all about their trip to Manitoulin Island in the far-off rugged and huge province of Ontario.

One morning about a year later Aunt Mary, Aunt Kathleen, Jacob, and Katie were having breakfast when Aunt Mary announced it was time for another trip. "Where should we go?" she asked.

The children were overjoyed. "Let's go see the Kangaroos and the Koala bears and the big wooly Sheep," Katie said. "Let's see where they live. Let's go to Australia!"

So off to Australia they went. Australia is much far-ther away from Alberta than O-N-T-A-R-I-O. But that's another story.

Dear reader,

We hope you enjoyed reading *Benjamin and Rumblechum*. Please take a moment to leave a review, even if it's a short one. Your opinion is important to us.

Discover more books by Kenna McKinnon at https://www.nextchapter.pub/authors/kenna-mckinnon

Want to know when one of our books is free or discounted? Join the newsletter at http://eepurl.com/bqqB3H

Best regards,
Kenna McKinnon, Emma Shirley Brinson and the Next Chapter Team

About the Authors

Kenna McKinnon is the author of *SpaceHive*, a middle grade sci-fi/fantasy novel published by Imajin Books; *The Insanity Machine*, a self-published memoir with co-author Austin Mardon, PhD, CM; and *DISCOVERY – a Collection of Poetry*, all released in 2012. Two of the mentioned books have recently been re-published by *Creativia/Next Chapter. BIGFOOT BOY: Lost on Earth*, was released in November 2013 by Mockingbird Lane Press. Her books are available in eBook and paperback worldwide on Amazon, Smashwords, Barnes & Noble, and in selected bookstores and public libraries.

Her interests/hobbies include occasional runner, volunteer, reading, writing, sporadic student of hatha yoga, ju-jitsu and kickboxing, weightlifting, and frequent walker. She lives in a high-rise bachelor suite in the trendy neighborhood of Oliver in the City of Edmonton. Her most memorable years were spent at the University of Alberta, where she graduated with Distinction with a degree in Anthropology (1975). She has lived successfully with schizophrenia for many years and is a member of the Writers' Guild of Alberta and the Canadian Authors

Association. She has three wonderful children and three grandsons.

Her author's blog: http://kennamckinnon.blogspot.com/
Facebook:
https://www.facebook.com/KennaMcKinnonAuthor
Twitter: http://www.twitter.com/KennaMcKinnon

Emma Shirley Brinson was born and raised in Alberta, Canada. She had the privilege of teaching in the field of Early Childhood Education for 37 years, retiring in 2009. Her interests are many: travelling, photography, gardening, reading, exercise, yoga, needlework, quilting, and spending time with family and friends. During 1982-83 Emma Shirley took a year off teaching to travel. It was on this trip she met Benjamin, who travelled with her and had many memorable and exciting adventures. Since then Benjamin has continued to travel. Emma Shirley presently lives in Edmonton, Alberta with her beloved purebred Persian cat, Freedom.

Aniela Abair is an artist/illustrator with published works in several media. This talented artist currently lives in Northern Michigan, USA, and specializes in pin-ups and superheroes. Sample artwork may be seen at http://www.anielaabair.deviantart.com/.

Lightning Source UK Ltd.
Milton Keynes UK
UKHW012134120421
381888UK00001B/111